THIS ANNUAL BELONGS TO

WHAT'S INSIDE ...

EGMONT

We bring stories to life

First published in 2013 by Egmont UK Limited, The Yellow Building, 1 Nicholas Road, London W11 4AN

Activities and story adaptations by Catherine Shoolbred. Designed by Claire Yeo and Cassie Benjamin.

Tree Fu Tom created by Daniel Bays.
Stories based on the episodes So Long Greenhorns written by Moya O'Shea, May The Best Berry Win by Douglas Wood, One For All by John Loy, Hovering Humblebugs by Andrew Emerson and Buzzworthy by Corey Powell.

BBC **FREMANTLE**MEDIA
ENTERPRISES

ISBN 978 1 4052 6766 3
54819/1
Printed in Italy

WELCOME

Welcome to the TREE FU TOM ANNUAL !

Read on to enjoy a world of magic, fun and friendship, as Tom has adventures with his friends in Treetopolis. Join in with the **BIG WORLD MAGIC** moves to help Tom save the day!

PARENTS' INFORMATION:

The **BIG WORLD MAGIC** movements are drawn from therapeutic techniques that assist and enhance physical and neurological development. The spells have been created to enable children to experience as many of the twelve key developmental movement skills as possible. The **TREE FU** movements improve stability and balance, which helps with early learning goals like dressing, eating and writing. They also teach spatial concepts like up, down, away from and into. **TREE FU TOM** encourages children to get involved and be active, all while having lots of **FUN!**

A CHANCE TO WIN £150 OF BOOK TOKENS!

See page 67 for details.

MEET THE GANG

TWIGS, the acorn guardian sprite, is Tom's best friend. He's always silly and funny!

ARIELA runs the Branch Ranch. She's strong and clever and loves to win!

SQUIRMTUM mines for magic sap in the sap tunnels and caverns of Treetopolis.

FLICKER, the glowing firefly, lives in his helmet.

TOM is an ordinary boy who uses *TREE FU MAGIC* to transform into a magical superhero! He goes on amazing adventures with his friends in Treetopolis.

ZIGZOO loves inventing machines to help others, but they often go wrong!

RICKETY, the friendly spider, teaches Tom and his friends to be amazing Squizzle players.

TREETOG is a wise Tree Spirit who teaches Tom and Twigs the ways of *TREE FU* in the Spell School at the castle.

PUFFY AND STINK are the mischievous Mushas! They cause lots of trouble in Treetopolis.

TREE FU MAGIC MOVES!

Do the moves to turn your magic powers on!

TIME FOR TREE FU!

To make Tree Fu spells do what you see.

1

Slide to the side.

2

And jump right back.

3

Hold your hands up high.

4

Spin around and reach up for the sky.

5

Now make a pose.

7

Touch your nose.

6

ARIELA FOLLOW THE LINES

Ariela is trying to lasso Teabiscuit to stop him causing trouble!

Follow the rope lines to see which one will capture him.

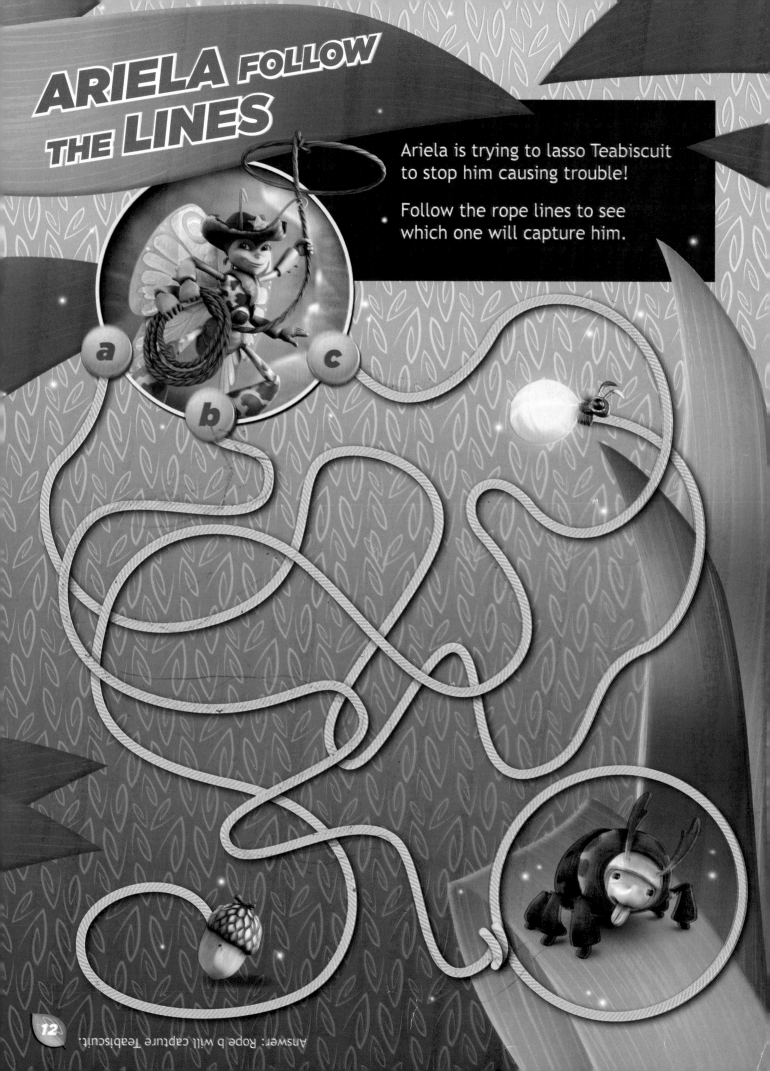

SO LONG, GREENHORNS!

Turn to page 10 to turn your magic powers on, so you're ready to help Tom!

Help read this story. Join in when you see a picture.

 Tom
 Twigs
 Ariela
 Squirmtum
 Zigzoo
 Treetog
 Teabiscuit

 and think learning spells is harder than ranch work. "Tree Fu is just word learning and funny moves," says , making  gasp.

"OK, let's swap jobs. You go to Spell School and we'll run the ranch!" say  and ..

"You greenhorns running my ranch?" laughs  . "You got yourself a deal!"

13

At the castle,  gives  a magic belt. "Use small movements to do this Tree Fu spell,"  says kindly. But  does big moves and her magic blasts a vase into the wall. SMASH! *Oh, no!*

At the ranch,  and  struggle to put berries into boxes and feed hungry aphids at the same time.  invents a machine to do both jobs for them.

shows a transportation spell,

but does it wrong and ends up inside a bottle!

"I miss my ranch," sighs sadly.

Things aren't going well at her ranch either.

 knocks Zigzoo's invention, so it starts

feeding the berries and putting the aphids into boxes!

The aphids cry and the berries grow bigger and

bigger. They're going to explode!

needs your help to float the berries away!

**It's time to do BIG WORLD MAGIC.
Are you ready? Tree Fu Go!**

THE BLOW A BUBBLE SPELL

Right copy me, into your spell pose!

Draw a big circle with one hand.

1

Make a bubble with both thumbs.

7

Make a bubble with your finger and thumb.

2

Bring your hands into the middle.

6

And turn them upside down.

Draw a big circle with your other hand.

3

Then float the bubbles into the air.

Make a bubble with your finger and thumb.

4

5

16

The **BIG WORLD MAGIC** bubbles lift the giant berries

high into the sky, where they explode safely.

stops the invention and settles the babies. Then

 does a magic spell to tidy up the hay, but

he accidentally traps in a hay bale!

Hungry knocks over ,

then chases him down the hill.

 messes up yet another spell and realises that

she prefers life on her ranch, even if it is hard work.

She thanks and flies back home.

Meanwhile, is still trying to catch .

"If we can get into the pen, will

follow," tells . He uses a magic lasso

to swing into the pen and closes the gate

after bounds in after him.

Just then,  arrives back at the ranch. She explains how hard she found Spell School.

"We had a tricky time on the ranch too," says  .

"We greenhorns think you're really clever to run it by yourself,"  adds.

"And you're real smart to learn all those spells," replies  .

"It's time for me to go,"  smiles.

"See you soon for another adventure!"

THE END

SHADOW MATCH

Draw lines to match Tom and his friends to their shadows.

1

2

3

4

a

b

c

d

WHAT CAN YOU SEE?

Look carefully at this picture, then answer the questions about it.

1. Who is next to?

   a. **b.** **c.**

2. Is Puffy's bow ...?
   a. blue **b.** yellow **c.** purple

3. Who is flying above ?

   a. **b.** **c.**

4. Who is standing next to ?

   a. **b.** **c.**

5. Who is looking at the Holopax on his wrist?

   a. **b.** **c.**

PUFFY AND STINK PUZZLE

The Mushas both want the trophy! Follow their trails to see who gets it!

PUFFY

STINK

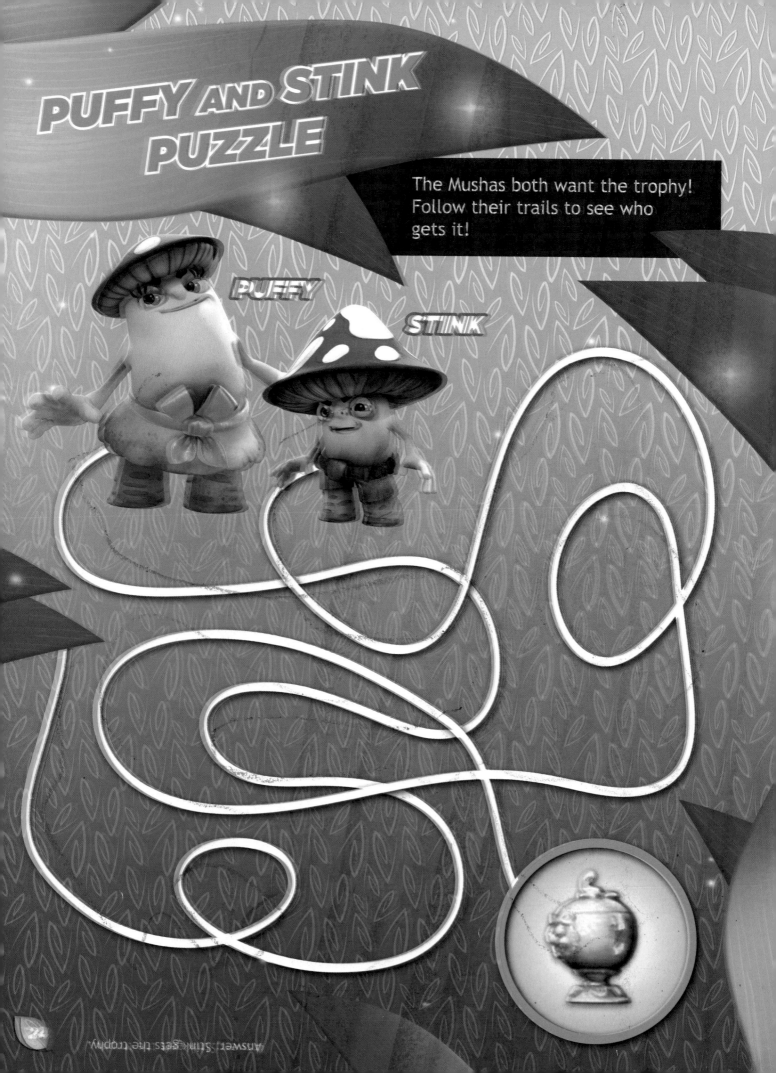

Answer: Stink gets the trophy.

MAY THE BEST BERRY WIN

Turn to page 10 to turn your magic powers on, so you're ready to help Tom!

It's the day of the Biggest Chuckleberry in Treetopolis contest! Twigs knows his tiny chuckleberry is too small to win and anyway, Ariela always wins the contest. But this year Puffy and Stink want to win it. They secretly pump all the juice out of Ariela's huge chuckleberry to make it tiny.

Ariela is shocked to find her deflated berry! Zigzoo uses his Size-o-Scope to make it big again, but Ariela wants to make it even bigger. Tom points out that would be cheating, but Ariela does it anyway. Her berry grows out of control and rolls towards the castle. Tom makes a magic shield to stop the berry just in time!

25

Ariela looks sadly at her smashed berry. Then Stink goes by with an ENORMOUS berry for the competition. Soon Treetog awards the winning trophy to Stink.

"I got what I deserved. Cheaters never win," Ariela says. But then she sees a rope under Stink's berry. Pulling it reveals that it's a pretend berry with Puffy hiding inside!

"I may not deserve the trophy, but you don't either, you cheated!" Ariela tells the Mushas, as she takes the trophy. Puffy chases Ariela and knocks into the Size-o-Scope, which makes Puffy grow huge!

Tom grabs the trophy and rushes to the top of the tower. But giant Puffy wants it back. She squashes all the competition berries as she follows him, then she starts climbing up the tower! "She's going to break it!" cries Twigs.

Tom needs your help to lift the heavy Size-o-Scope to the top of the tower, to change Puffy back to her normal size.

**It's time to do BIG WORLD MAGIC.
Are you ready? Tree Fu Go!**

27

THE MEGA ATTRACTER SPELL

Right copy me, into your spell pose!

BIG WORLD MAGIC

Step forwards, reach and pull back.

1

Other foot, step, reach and pull back.

2

Now reach up and pull down. That's really good!

5

Make a big circle back with one arm and a big circle back with the other arm.

3

Make a big circle back with both arms.

4

Do the same moves again, then ...

Clap and say "Mega Attracter" to send the magic to me!

6

Yes, we did it! Thanks for your help.

29

Twigs leaps onto the Size-o-Scope as the Big World Magic lifts it to the top of the tower. Then he fires the magic beam, which shrinks Puffy back to normal size. She slides down the tower and lands on Stink — SPLAT! They quickly run away. Tom and his friends start cleaning up.

"Maybe mopping up this mess will remind me cheating doesn't pay," smiles Ariela.

Puffy has squashed all the berries so it looks like no one will win the competition. But then Twigs realises he still has his little chuckleberry, it's the last one left!

"You win, Twigs!" chuckles Treetog. Twigs laughs and eats his chuckleberry, which giggles in his tummy.

"Maybe I shouldn't have eaten that; I feel a little funny!" he chuckles.

"Nice one, Twigs!" says Tom, and everyone laughs!

THE END

DOT-TO-DOT SIZE-O-SCOPE

Join the dots to complete the Size-o-Scope. Then colour it in!

SQUIRMTUM MAZE

Help Squirmtum find his way through the maze to see Ariela's baby bugs.

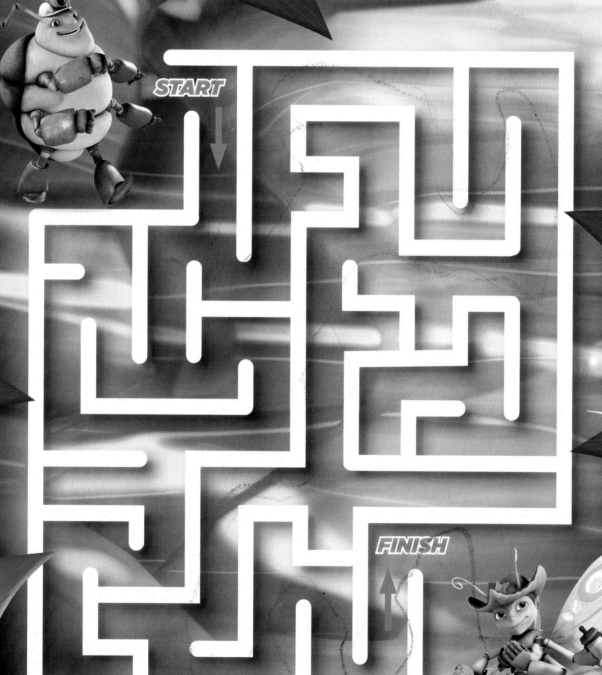

START

FINISH

Answer:

BUZZWORTHY

Turn to page 10 to turn your magic powers on, so you're ready to help Tom!

One day, Ariela is feeding her ladybirds with nectar. "They're always hungry," she tells Tom and Twigs, who help her to collect more nectar from the flowers.

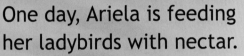

Tom casts a Shake It Spell to shake the nectar out of the flowers, but a swarm of bees starts taking the nectar to make honey for their hive! "Hey! They're my flowers, go somewhere else!" Ariela cries.

Tom and Twigs try to keep the bees away from the flowers, but they are too fast. Ariela tries to lasso one to stop it taking her nectar, but she's pulled into the sky and taken to their hive.

Tom and Twigs can't reach Ariela, as there are too many bees flying in their way.

Tom uses a Go Slow Spell to slow down the bees so they can rescue Ariela from the hive. They then collect as much nectar as they can before the bees speed up again.

But before they can collect many cups of nectar, the bees speed up and start taking them again. Ariela still doesn't want to share, so she chases after them. But she crashes into the hive causing a massive flood of honey!

"Our home!" cry the bees.
"And my ranch!" says Ariela.
"We need to work together to save them," says Tom.
"You're right!" say the bees. "What shall we do?"
"Ariela, bees, you fix the hive. Twigs, you protect the ladybirds and I'll use Big World Magic to stop the honey," Tom replies.

Tom needs your help with BIG WORLD MAGIC *to make a Lifting Wind Spell. Are you ready? Tree Fu Go!*

THE LIFTING WIND SPELL

Right copy me, into your spell pose!

BIG WORLD MAGIC

Palms together, arms straight. Then squat down.

1

Arms up. Circle your whole body one way.

6

Circle your arms one way.

2

Then circle them back

5

Then circle them back the other way.

3

Stand up. Circle your arms one way.

4

Then circle your whole body back. Great!

7

Do the same moves again. Then ...

Clap your hands and say "Lifting Wind" to send the magic to me!

8

Yes, we did it!
Thanks for
your help!

The spell lifts the honey back into the hive, and Ariela and the bees stick it back together.

"We're going to be OK! Wahay!" smiles Twigs.

"Hip, hip, hooray!" everyone says together.

"From now on we'd always like to share," the bees tell Ariela, as they give her some honey.

"Me too!" says Ariela. "There's plenty of nectar to go around and this honey is good!" she smiles as she shares it out.

"Sweet!" replies Twigs, licking his honey-covered lips, and everyone laughs.

THE END

COLOURING TOM

Add colour to Tom, so he can fly off and join his friends.

TREE FU BINGO!

Play Tree Fu Bingo with a friend. Each image relates to a different action. Throw a dice then do the move that matches the number. The winner is the first player to tick off all six moves!

Player 1
Tree Fu Go!

Throw a dice, then do the moves that match the number.

1	**2**	**3**	**4**	**5**	**6**
Hum loudly and **step** slowly around the room.	**Hold** your tummy and **chuckle** like a chuckleberry!	**Jump** up and pretend to catch a **Squizzle!**	**Flap** your arms and say **"Buzz!"** like a bee.	Say **"Yee-ha!"** and pretend to swing a **lasso.**	Pretend to be really SMALL then really **BIG!**

Player 2
Tree Fu Go!

SPOT THE DIFFERENCE

It's a lovely day in Treetopolis and Tom's having fun with his friends!

1

Colour in a leaf as you find each change!

These pictures look the same but there are 6 differences in picture 2. Can you spot them all?

Answers: Flicker has disappeared, the school spire is orange, the leaves are missing, Stink has appeared, the window is blue and Twigs' sapstone has disappeared.

THE REAL ZIGZOO!

Which shadow matches this picture of Zigzoo exactly?

a

b

c

Answer: b matches.

WHO'S WHO?

Draw lines to match the close-ups to the right characters.

a

b

c

d

1

2

3

4

45

HOVERING HUMBLEBUGS

Turn to page 10 to turn your magic powers on, so you're ready to help Tom!

It's the day of Treetog's Magic and Movements tests! Tom gets full marks in the movement test. Then in the magic test, he has to float a chuckleberry through some rings and drop it into a basket. But it smashes on the ground.

SPLAT!

"Oh no!" cries Tom, "I wanted to show Treetog I could do that perfectly!"

"Hey! What's that humming noise?" asks Twigs.

They look up and see a family of Hovering Humblebugs above them.

"They stop here every year, hovering high above Treetopolis as they migrate to their new home," says Treetog. "I've always wanted to hear their beautiful song," she adds.

Tom wants to impress Treetog by getting the bugs to sing for her.

"That will show her that I can do something perfectly," he tells Twigs.

But Tom flies into the Humblebug Queen and knocks her crown off. It smashes on a branch and the pieces scatter across Treetopolis!

"I've got to fix this!" Tom cries, flying down to find the crown pieces. The Queen's bugs chase after him.

Tom calls Zigzoo for help. He brings his Super Seek-a-Matic invention to help find the crown pieces.

"If I can find them and mend the crown, the Humblebug Queen might sing for Treetog!" Tom tells him.

The Humblebugs also want to find the crown pieces, but Tom's determined to find them first. The friends race around in Zigzoo's wagon picking up crown pieces as they go. But, as the bugs catch up with them, Zigzoo takes a sharp turn and his wagon ends up stuck at the edge of Rickety's gorge.

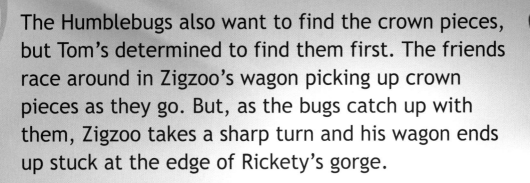

"We're doomed!" says Twigs.
"We can jump across with Big World Magic!" Tom replies.
"We're saved!" says Twigs.
"Get a good run up, Zigzoo, and I'll do the rest," Tom tells him ...

Tom needs your help to lift the wagon across the gorge. It's time to do BIG WORLD MAGIC. *Are you ready? Tree Fu Go!*

MEGA POWER BOOST SPELL

Right copy me, into your spell pose!

Move one arm across, then the other arm across.

1

Roll your arms ....

5

Close then open your fingers on each hand.

2

Reach across and touch the floor.

3

Now make a big star.

4

... and jump into the air. Brilliant!

6

Do the same moves again, then ...

Clap and say "Mega Power Boost" to send the magic to me!

7

Yes, we did it! Thanks for your help!

With Big World Magic power, the wagon leaps across the deep gorge. Tom cheers as he finds the last crown piece and, using magic, makes it whole again. When he sees the chasing Humblebugs are stuck in a web, he uses magic to quickly free them.

"Please take the crown back to the Queen and tell her I'm sorry," says Tom.

Later, Tom tells Treetog about how his 'perfect plan' to get the Humblebugs to sing for her went wrong.

"We can't always do things perfectly," Treetog says. "You helped others in trouble, I'm impressed," she adds.

Then the Humblebugs and their Queen fly down and thank Tom by singing for him and Treetog.

"Wonderful! Well done Tom," says Treetog, as the Humblebugs fly off to their new home.

THE END

COPY COLOUR TWIGS

Use the little picture as a guide to colour in Twigs!

COUNT FROM 1 TO 10

Look carefully at the picture, then count these ten objects.

Answer:

Find and count these objects.

1
2
3
4
5
6
7
8
9
10

55

ONE FOR ALL

Turn to page 10 to turn your magic powers on, so you're ready to help Tom!

Tom, Twigs, Squirmtum and Ariela are at Squizzle practice with Rickety before a big Squizzle Competition. But they aren't playing very well.

"To be a great team you need to speak to each other, listen and focus," Rickety tells them. "Or you could just use the Enchanted Squizzle!" he adds.

Everyone wants to know more about the Enchanted Squizzle. Rickety tells them that the team who finds it and wins it from the Squizzle Master will play perfectly and be unbeatable.

Tom and his team are determined to get it!

Rickety says they'll have to face special challenges to get the Enchanted Squizzle. The first challenge is 'seek and defeat the purple weed'. Tom sets off to find it, but Rickety reminds him he's part of a team.

"Let's find it together," Tom says, and the others agree.

When they find it, the weed shoots seeds at them. But by working together, they defeat it. They then find a clue that leads to the sap caverns.

They help each other to the next clue, which tells them to 'focus'. They have to step on footprints that lead to the Enchanted Squizzle. But when Squirmtum stops thinking about where he's walking and steps off them, the floor falls away! Tom uses Tree Fu Magic to make stepping stones, so Squirmtum can get to safety.

They find the Enchanted Squizzle in a spooky cavern. Their last challenge is set by the Squizzle Master — a mysterious voice that echoes around the cavern. They have to use the Enchanted Squizzle to hit lots of wingseeds and they play perfectly! Then Rickety steps out of the shadows — he's the Squizzle Master! But then the ceiling rumbles and boulders start falling on them!

Tom needs your help to freeze the falling boulders. It's time to do BIG WORLD MAGIC. Are you ready? Tree Fu Go!

THE SUPER FREEZE SPELL

Right copy me, into your spell pose!

With your hands push from side to side.

1

Keep going FAST.

2

3 ... 2 ... 1. Freeze! Well done!

3

swing your arms forwards like you're swimming.

4

Keep going FAST.

5

3 ... 2 ... 1. FREEZE! That's really great!

6

Do the same moves again, then ...

Clap and say "Super Freeze" to send the magic to me!

7

Yes, we did it! Thanks for your help!

61

The Big World Magic stops the falling boulders and, as a team, they use the Enchanted Squizzle to smash them to dust. But as they hit the last one, the Enchanted Squizzle snaps!

"Oh, no!" they cry. "We'll never play well again."

"Yes you will," smiles Rickety. "There's no such thing as an Enchanted Squizzle, it is the same Squizzle you played with this morning. Teamwork was your special power!"

"Go team!" they cheer.

"Thanks for being the best coach ever, Rickety!" says Tom.

And they all shout together: "It's all for one ... and one for all!"

THE END

MATCHING PAIRS

Can you find the matching pairs below?

TREETOPOLIS GAME

HOW TO PLAY:

You need a dice and a counter for each player. Take turns to roll the dice and do the moves as you make your way around the board. The first to the finish wins!

START

1 TURN TO PAGE 10 TO DO THE TREE FU MOVES

2

3 TOUCH YOUR KNEES

11

12 MAKE A BIG CIRCLE WITH BOTH ARMS

13

14 REACH UP HIGH, THEN DOWN LOW

15

16 HANDS TOGETHER AND SQUAT

17

18 DO THREE BIG STAR JUMPS

4 SLIDE TO BOTH SIDES

5 →

6 HOP TWICE FORWARDS THEN BACK

7 ↷

8 REACH UP TO THE SKY

9 ←

10 CLAP YOUR HANDS AND SPIN AROUND

19 →

20 WAVE GOODBYE TO TOM AND FRIENDS!

FINISH

65

GOODBYE!

"THANKS FOR HELPING ME IN TREETOPOLIS. SEE YOU SOON FOR ANOTHER ADVENTURE. BYE FOR NOW!"

READER SURVEY

We'd love to know what you think about your Tree Fu Tom Annual.
Ask a grown-up to help you fill in this form and post it to the address
at the end by 28th February 2014, or you can fill in the survey online at:
www.egmont.co.uk/treefutomsurvey2014
One lucky reader will win £150 of book tokens!
Five runners-up will receive a £25 book token each.

NATIONAL BOOK tokens

1. Who bought this annual?

☐ Me
☐ Parent/guardian
☐ Grandparent
☐ Other (please specify)

_____

2. Why did they buy it?

☐ Christmas present
☐ Birthday present
☐ I'm a collector
☐ Other (please specify)

_____

3. What are your favourite parts of the annual?

Stories	☐	Really like	☐	Like	☐ Don't like
Picture puzzles	☐	Really like	☐	Like	☐ Don't like
Character profiles	☐	Really like	☐	Like	☐ Don't like
Colouring	☐	Really like	☐	Like	☐ Don't like
Games	☐	Really like	☐	Like	☐ Don't like

4. Do you think the stories are too long, too short or about right?

☐ Too long
☐ Too short
☐ About right

_____

5. Do you think the activities are too hard, too easy or about right?

☐ Too hard
☐ Too easy
☐ About right

_____

6. Apart from Tom and Twigs, who are your favourite characters?

1. _____
2. _____
3. _____

7. Which other annuals do you like?

1. _____
2. _____
3. _____

8. What is your favourite ...

1. ... app or website? _____
2. ... console game? _____
3. ... magazine? _____
4. ... book? _____

9. What are your favourite TV programmes?

1. _____
2. _____
3. _____

10. Would you like to get the Tree Fu Tom Annual again next year?

☐ Yes
☐ No
Why? _____

GOOD LUCK!

Thank you!
(Please ask your parent/guardian to complete)

Child's name: _____ Age: _____ Boy/Girl

Parent/guardian name: _____

Parent/guardian signature: _____

Parent/guardian email address: _____

Daytime telephone number: _____

☐ Please send me the Egmont Monthly Catch-Up Newsletter.
Please cut out this form and post to: Tree Fu Tom Annual Reader Survey,
Egmont UK Limited, The Yellow Building, 1 Nicholas Road, London, W11 4AN